Published 1985 by Derrydale Books,
Distributed by Crown Publishers, Inc.
Printed in Hungary
ISBN 0–517–47106X
HGFEDCBA

# Rip van Winkle

## Retold & Illustrated by John Patience

Derrydale Books
New York

Long ago in North America, in a village at the foot of the Catskill Mountains, lived a man called Rip van Winkle. Rip was a good-natured man who was always ready to lend his neighbors a helping hand, or listen to their troubles. He was very popular with everyone, but best of all Rip liked to spend his time with his little daughter and the other village children. He taught them to fly kites, carved them boats to sail and told them long stories of ghosts, witches and Indians.

Unfortunately, Rip's wife did not share other people's good opinion of her husband. She had a terrible temper and nagged poor Rip from morning till night. "You are always willing to help other people," she complained, "but you will never do a stroke of work at home. Our farm is falling into ruins and your family is dressed in rags." To escape from his wife's temper, Rip would often take his gun and go hunting in the Catskill Mountains.

One day, on one of his hunting expeditions, Rip was surprised to hear someone calling his name. "Rip van Winkle! Rip van Winkle!" Rip turned and saw a strange little man toiling up the mountainside. He was bending under the weight of a barrel that he carried on his back. The stranger asked Rip to help him, and though he was a little frightened, Rip took the barrel and lifted it on to his shoulder.

The stranger showed the way and Rip went on ahead, clambering up a narrow gully. As he climbed he heard a sound like distant thunder. It made him feel rather uneasy. Presently they arrived at a level clearing. There, to Rip's astonishment, he saw a number of other strangely dressed little men. They were playing a game that looked like bowling, and it was the noise of the balls rolling which Rip had mistaken for thunder!

When the dwarves noticed Rip they stopped their game and began to stare at him. They stared so hard that Rip's knees began to knock together and his heart to pound.

The little men took the barrel from Rip and filled their flagons from it, after which they returned to their game. Eventually Rip's fear left him and, as no one was taking any notice of him, and he was feeling thirsty, he decided to try the drink himself. He filled a large bottle

and took a drink from it. The flavor was excellent, but the more he drank the more thirsty he became.

After a while, the dwarves did stop their game and the one who appeared to be their commander came over to watch Rip, who, by this time, was feeling very drowsy.

At last Rip's senses were overpowered, the faces of
the little men swam before his eyes, his head began to
nod and he fell into a deep, deep sleep.

When Rip awoke, it was a bright and sunny morning. "Surely," he thought, "I have not slept here all night." He looked around for signs of the little men, but they were nowhere to be seen. Stranger still, Rip found that brambles had tangled themselves around him while he slept and his clothes had become tattered and torn.

Slowly Rip struggled to his feet, his back was aching and his legs were stiff. With great difficulty he began to make his way down the mountain. To his astonishment everything seemed different; the paths had become overgrown and mountain streams now bubbled and flowed where there had not even been a trickle of water before.

When he reached the village, he met a number of people, but no one he recognized; this surprised him because he thought he knew everyone who lived in his village. These people were dressed in a new fashion and they stared at Rip and whispered about him as he passed. The dogs chased after Rip, barking at him as if he were a stranger.

It was not easy for Rip to find his way home. The streets were all different and new buildings had sprung up everywhere. "Can it be," he thought, "that all these changes have happened overnight?" At last Rip stood in front of his own house, but he could hardly believe his eyes. It was in ruins and looked as if it had not been lived in for years!

Rip wandered away feeling very puzzled. Suddenly he caught sight of himself in a shop window. He gasped; his reflection was that of a very old man with a long white beard! No wonder people had stared, no wonder his legs were so stiff. Now he realised that he must have slept for a great deal longer than one night — more like a hundred years. Perhaps there would not be a single person left in the village who would remember him.

By this time a large crowd had gathered around Rip. "I'm Rip van Winkle," he cried. "Doesn't anyone remember me?" Most of the people thought the old man must be mad. But then a young woman came out of the crowd and took him by the arm. "You must be my grandfather," she said. "I was told the story by my mother of how you disappeared in the mountains."

Rip's granddaughter told him of how his wife had died and his daughter had moved away, but she invited him to live with her and her family. Rip soon settled in happily, and delighted in sitting his grandchildren on his knee and telling them of his adventure in the magical Catskill Mountains.